Marie

Written By: Sara Kjeldsen

Copyright 2020 Sara Kjeldsen

Cover Design By: Adrijus from Rocking Book Covers

ISBN: 9798621061050

I knew that I was different from most people even when I was a small child. I never cried. I never wanted to be coddled. The first time I remember wanting to crush someone was on the daycare playground when I was four. There was a little boy one year younger than me. I still remember how his hair was so light that it reminded me of the sun. I've never liked the sun. He was small not just in body, but in mind. A gentle creature who needed to be conquered by someone stronger. Me.

I dropped my toys as I watched him play under a big tractor tire. I walked over to him and kicked him in the side. Hard. His pained cries didn't make me want to stop as he fell into the gravel. I didn't want it to end. I wanted him to cry more. I pushed him hard into the tire's crevice. He cried again, not bothering to fight me back. I shoved his head into the warm rubber. One of the early childhood educators saw what I was doing and moved me away from the victim. They told me I was cruel; they forced me to apologize to my crying little blond toy. I didn't care what they thought of me and I didn't regret it. I was suspended from the playground for a month.

I am now a woman in my thirties sitting by a pool in my black swimsuit. I wear a hat to protect my smooth, well-moisturized face from sun damage as I read a magazine. Black sunglasses shield my eyes from the brightness. I've always hated direct sunlight because it makes me aggressive. Splashing draws my attention away from an article on fall fashion's economic influences. I look over at the pool.

Something small and brown is struggling in the blue water. One of the baby bunnies has fallen in again. I stand up and watch the little ripples stretch out from the drowning creature as it tries in vain to get out of its trap. I walk up to it until my feet reach the pool's edge.

The tiny rabbit is fighting with all its might to survive, but it isn't crying the way most of them do when they are trapped in there. I roll up my magazine and use it to push the bunny's head below the water's surface. I move my hand away and its head bops above the surface again. Now it screams. I hate how hideous it sounds. I push it under the water again to drown out the noise.

"Is everything alright?" calls an annoyingly familiar voice.

It is the pool boy. The skin on my face becomes hot as I quickly move away from the drowning bunny and cover my mouth.

"Help me, please!" I cry. "I'm trying to save this bunny, but I'm scared it will bite me!"

I step aside as he quickly rushes over and grabs the thing with his bare hands. He lifts it out of the water. It looks so small in his grasp. It stops shrieking as it gasps for air. He walks over to the flower garden and lets it go. Rage fills my veins as I watch him handle the meaningless thing with such care. He's robbed me of my enjoyment for the afternoon. He is not supposed to be here at this time of day.

He turns back to me with a big smile on his face. He reminds me so much of a golden retriever – happy, dumb, and people-pleasing. He is twenty-two with sandy hair, big brown eyes, and a fit body. He hasn't taken off his shirt yet, but he looks delicious in his shorts and tank top. My physical attraction to him settles my anger, but it doesn't make me want to push him into the pool any less.

I force a smile. "You're a hero. Thank you for helping me."

He grins wider. I wonder how someone can always look so happy. What is he hiding?

"Those poor little guys have so much going against them. I'm happy to help," he says.

"Why are you here so early today?" I ask, feeling my smile waver.

He seems to sense my displeasure as his untimely arrival; his grin drops. "I'm sorry if I've overstepped my boundaries, Mrs. Robson. It's just that Mr. Robson said I could come to your place a little early to work on my assignment for school. I don't have Wi-Fi where I'm living right now and it's pretty noisy there"

"I see."

It is just like Mr. Robson to make decisions without consulting me. Corey Patrick Robson is his full name. He's the big shot pilot with hundreds of friends. We met on a dating app last year. Six months after our first date, I was able to get him to propose to me with a stunning diamond ring and our wedding was soon after in Dubai.

"It's okay that I'm here, right?" asks the pool boy. "I mean, I'd never want to make you feel uncomfortable or anything."

His face is now beat red. His awkwardness is grating my nerves. Why can't he just do his job and shut up?

"Of course, you can study here before you clean the pool," I say sweetly, walking past him. "Don't mind me. I'm just the housewife."

"Thank you, Mrs. Robson."

I exhale loudly as he leaves. My magazine is ruined from dipping it in the water and I didn't even get to watch the rabbit die. What a waste of pretty paper. I toss it in the trash and go up to my room to shower. We have a double date this evening with my husband's colleague and his wife.

I am grateful Corey is a pilot. It is why I have a

beautiful house and the luxury of sitting by the pool reading fashion magazines on hot days. I could work, but I have other things I'd rather do. My beauty routine is a part-time job itself. I go to the spa twice per week for skin treatments to keep my skin soft, smooth, and dewy. I go to the salon to have my nails done once per week and I get my dark roots touched up every two weeks so my blonde hair never looks the least bit cheap. My workout routines are intensive and regular. I train like a Victoria's Secret model, but I eat well to prevent myself from becoming too skinny.

My husband loves me only because I am beautiful. I need to be stunning at all times. That way he will give me whatever I want in return. This existence of mine will vanish if I begin to look unremarkable in any way.

I can't be replaced before I kill him.

The dinner conversation is contrived as usual, but I make a game out of fake laughing every time Corey's friend tells a lame joke. His wife has less personality than he does. We manage to avoid speaking with one another for most of the night, allowing our husbands to have the spotlight. I wonder if she's as bored as I am. Maybe she's planning to kill her beloved, too. I study her for a few moments. She smiles with her eyes and seems genuinely interested in the men's conversation. She works full-time at an office downtown and volunteers at a children's charity every Sunday. Her dress bothers me. The cut is a little too loose on her trim frame. Crow's feet already appear around her eyes and she is no older than me. Her reputation is that she'll move heaven and earth to accommodate her friends and loved ones. She does not seem clever enough to plan a murder. Selfless people are the dumbest ones of all.

When we return home, the pool boy is just leaving through the front door.

"Thank you both and good night!" he says quickly, rushing past us.

Corey chuckles. "See ya later, kid."

"Shouldn't he have been gone hours ago?" I ask.

"I told him he could stay until we get back. He's a good kid from a not-so-good background. I'm happy to open our home to him when he needs it."

I glare at him. "This is our home and you let him stay there alone? We hardly know him. Why do you like him so much?"

"Brad joined our men's soccer team recently and we hit it off. He's a great asset to the team. You and I have a big house and no kids ... yet. We might as well let a friend enjoy it."

I clench my fists. This is not acceptable. Having a person who shows up at our house unexpectedly will complicate my life tremendously. Corey has given me a good reason to end him. He has allowed an intruder to invade my palace. Soon, I will have all his money and I can move to a nicer home where no one can bother me. Once he's dead.

The next day after Corey leaves, I start to set my plans in motion. I need to act fast before he and Brad form a stronger bond. I want it to be a clean kill, but I need to do it outside of the house because of Brad. I fume at the thought of that boy having keys to our home. Corey has no idea who Brad is. For all we know, he has plans to kill us and take all our money.

I go with my idea to lead Corey out to the woods

after drugging his drink. He will follow me willingly thinking it's some kinky new thing I want to try. The method in which I will kill him is still up in the air. I could choose from many interesting methods. There have been wolves passing through the forest behind our house recently. They often do at this time of year. I think of attaching raw meat to his corpse to attract them to him, but the disgusting imagery of what would follow prevents me from doing so. I like imagining disturbing things, but I hate filth. The idea of a mess in the woods so close to my home will drive me to madness. Besides, someone might see it if they happen to be walking close by. There are trails all around that forest.

"Scratch that idea. A clean murder it will be," I whisper to myself.

I call one of my contacts on a payphone. His name is Steve. He's a thirty-something millionaire who I met at a party last year. He was keen to hook me up with the best drugs last time we spoke. Now is his chance. When he answers my call, I ask if I can fly a kite with him. That is code for buying ketamine.

We meet in the park after sunset and make our exchange without a word, but I do not miss the curious look he gives me before walking back to his vehicle. Now that I have the ketamine and a small bag of syringes in my purse, I can get rid of Corey.

The next morning, I am greeted by Brad's sickening smile by the pool. Why the hell is he so happy? The kid is so poor that he has to leech off his new friend for food, a study space, and Wi-Fi. If another small animal falls into the pool, he will be sure to save it. I pout and sit down on the soft chair by the pool. I am not going to stay away from my favourite place just because the pool boy is there.

"Good morning, Mrs. Robson," he says.

"Morning, bitch," I say under my breath

I wave at him with a wide grin. He smiles. It doesn't seem like he heard me.

He is going to pay one day for trespassing on my peace. I flip through another magazine in annoyance. A sudden splash brings me out of my momentary fantasy world. My heart races as I sit up. How I crave to relish in that little one's tortuous death by drowning.

11

"Poor little guy," I hear Brad say as he moves toward the edge of the pool.

He bends down and helps another bunny out of the water. It claws at him as he lifts it out. He drops it instinctively and it scurries toward the bushes. His hair looks golden in the sunlight as he watches the little rabbit hop away. Brad's gentle disposition is like a warm summer breeze. I hate him for that.

He examines the red scratches on his arms. I don't want to help him. I am glad he is suffering for intruding on my morning.

"Let me help you clean those battle wounds, young man," I say with a syrupy tone. "Those scratches must hurt."

"I don't think you're old enough to call me 'young man'," he says with a chuckle.

I raise an eyebrow at him. I like it when people speak the truth. He smiles bashfully as his eyes scan my figure. I am wearing a red bikini. I don't bother to cover up with my sarong as I lead him into the house. I have worked hard to maintain my tight, svelte figure so I should show it off.

I find a first aid kit and give him the items needed to clean the little wounds on his skin.

"You're sweet, Mrs. Robson," he says.

Oh, how I want him to think of me that way. I utter a soft laugh. "You're the kind one saving those innocent little animals from drowning."

He responds to the sound of my voice by moving closer. He stares at my lips. I can't help but smile at him admiring me, but I'd prefer him to view me from a distance. Men will always respect a woman more when she seems unattainable to them.

"Now, off you go," I say, playfully shooing him out of the room. "Time for you to go back to work."

"Yes, ma'am," he says, face flushed.

I go up to my room to plan out the rest of Corey's murder. I can't have that blushing fool distracting me. If only I hadn't misplaced the paper that has my brain storming on it. I am not normally so careless. The words I wrote on it are so abstract that if someone were to find it and read it, they likely wouldn't suspect it as anything more than random scribblings. I am just a stupid housewife, after all.

I sit on my bed and go over the different murder scenarios in my head then I determine the risks for each one. I can't wait much longer. I will have to act while everyone still believes I am Corey's sweet little wife. I can only hide my true nature for so long. People would be safer if they stayed away from me, but some of them insist on overstepping my boundaries. It is their own fault for getting killed.

-2-

The next morning, I start to prepare myself as though I am going out to a fancy gala. I need to look perfect on this day. I will make Corey fall in love with me even more. I visit the salon to get my nails done then I ask my stylist for a fresh icy blonde tone in my hair. After that, I get my makeup done at a Dior counter by my favourite makeup artist. She is known for creating soft and sultry looks and she never fails to meet my expectations.

I pick up a designer floor-length red dress from Sancta Sophia and return home to have a bubble bath. After I am thoroughly cleansed, I dry off, moisturize, and slip into my feminine armour. I pose in front of the mirror in my new gown. I love how it fits my slender body like a glove, emphasizing my small waist.

I hear Corey come through the door. I fill the needle with ketamine from the bottle and put it in my purse. I walk downstairs with a sweet smile on my face to greet my husband. As I step toward the entranceway, it is Brad who appears around the corner.

"What are you doing here?" I demand.

"Corey said he's going to be late because of a meeting at the airport tonight so he said I could fix myself some dinner if I want to."

My jaw drops open as hot rage surges through my veins. Since when does Corey stay late at work? That is a first. My limbs tremble. I want to hurt Brad for his audacity to walk into my home so late without Corey home.

"I wasn't aware that we haven taken in a foster child," I remark.

He takes a step back. "You're a hard one to read, Mrs. Robson. Sometimes you seem welcoming, other times I think you want me to leave. Is there something about me that offends you or something?"

He has a lot of nerve stepping into my home asking me that. He has crossed the line. I want to see him lying helpless on the floor in front of me.

"This is not your home, Brad," I state.

He needs to leave, but he's too foolish for that.

"The reason why I came here is because I saw something you wrote. I don't think you wanted me to see it. I wanted to ask you about it."

"How did you find it? Were you sneaking around?"

"A certain piece of paper fell out of your magazine when you didn't notice. I know I should have given it to you, but I was curious about what you were writing, so I kept it. To be honest, it looks like a murder plan."

What an idiot. I don't blink. I don't feel nervous. I am better than him and I always will be even if I made that clumsy move.

"What are you talking about?" I ask, widening my eyes in mock ignorance.

He clears his throat, fiddling with his hands. He looks very anxious. I like that. His confidence is waning.

"The morning I caught you trying to drown the little rabbit," he begins, "I wondered what would possess such a beautiful and seemingly kind woman to do that."

I stifle the anger rising within me and meet his gaze. "Is that it, Brad? You think I was trying to drown a rabbit and now you think I'm a murderer."

"I'm studying psychology with hopes of being a psychiatrist one day. You seem to be good at faking empathy when you want to and you also seem to enjoy hurting things."

"Oh, so you're a smart guy, are you? What is my diagnosis, Bradley?"

I almost laugh at him.

"You plan to kill someone," he says.

There it is.

"That is a bold claim to make about the lady of the house."

He takes a step closer to me and his gaze travels below my chin to my cleavage. "I know what I saw you write, but I can keep it a secret if you promise not to do it."

His smirk returns as he inches closer to me. Where did he get such arrogance from? I don't need him to keep any of my secrets. Brad may be stronger in body, but I am more cunning. My power surpasses his and always will.

"You will regret this," I say, turning around and

digging into my purse for the bottle and syringe.

"I can help you, Marie," he says softly. "Sit down and talk to me about what you've been going through. I will listen."

I pull out the syringe filled with ketamine and jab his arm with it, quickly injecting the drug into his body. He draws back in shock. I smile.

"Don't ever let your guard down, but I guess that lesson is too late for you now."

"What ... why did you ..."

He visibly weakens as he stumbles away from me. He is in flight mode, but it won't be enough for him to get away. I don't act. I just watch. He makes it to the door, but he struggles to turn the knob as the toxin works quickly through his bloodstream. He falls to the floor, struggling to get back up. I wait. He will be out soon.

When he lies still on the floor, I walk over to the big knife resting on the counter. I long to slice up his smooth skin, but it would leave too much of a mess. I grab him under the armpits and drag him across the floor to the back door. I am fit, but it is mostly from cardio and Pilates workouts. I am sweating and winded by the time I pull him over to the pool's edge, fully aware of the fact that I need to increase my upper body strength. I use my foot to push his limp body into the water. He floats for a few moments before sinking below the surface.

I watch as his lean body descends to the pool's floor. He is oblivious to the fact that he is drowning. I spared him from that torture. I smile at the poetic nature of his death. He stopped me from toying with my prey, so I made him take its place.

I walk around the perimeter of the pool as he sinks. I decide to wait for half an hour just to be sure he's perfectly dead. I slip out of my red gown and dive into the water. I swim to the bottom of the pool, grab his lifeless body, and pull him with all my strength up to the surface. His wet skin glows in the moonlight. He is cold to the touch. I hold his corpse above the gently disturbed waters. This is the beautiful life I have taken. He is helpless in my arms and I am breathless.

I bring him close to the edge, push myself up, and use all my might to pull him out of the water. I walk back into the house wet and shivering then I grab the phone out of my purse to call Steve. He answers and sounds surprised that I called.

"Hey, I need help moving a body from my home," I say.

"A body?" he asks, but he doesn't sound overly surprised.

"Yes. Please hurry. I need this dealt with as soon as possible."

He once joked about having all the chemicals needed to properly dispose of a body. Sometimes when people make jokes about something, there is some truth to it. When Steve arrives at the front door, I have already showered and changed into my black Adidas jogging outfit.

My red dress is hanging up in my closet. I will take it to the dry cleaners in the morning. I have deleted the video footage off all the cameras and turned them off to prevent further footage until Steve has left with the body. I wiped the floors, counters, and all the surfaces he touched. It was an easy murder.

When Steve knocks at the door, I waste no time

leading him to the pool. He lifts the fit but dead twenty-two-year-old body off the cement. I lead him around the house so that more water is not dripped all over the floors. He puts the corpse into the back of his black Ford Explorer; he was careful to park in the dark off to the side of the driveway. He flashes me a wry grin. Steve is no stranger to dead bodies. I can tell.

"I admit that I didn't originally think of you as that type of girl."

"How much do you want for this? I owe you."

He grins. "Meet me at my place tomorrow for dinner."

"I'll see you tomorrow night then. Things should go smoothly after this. We've covered all our bases."

He winks. "It's your murder. I'm just taking care of the disposal."

I feel the air around me chill even though it is a warm summer night. I don't expect this odd sensation. I have done the world a favour. Brad is an idiot and he deserves to be dead.

3

I awaken the next morning feeling lighter than usual.
The annoyance from yesterday is gone. No one will
interrupt my mornings by the pool for a while. Brad
will never be back. I perform my usual skin care
regime, put on a white slip dress, and style my hair in
a quick updo. I go downstairs for my first cup of
coffee of the day. Corey is sitting at the table reading
a paper. He greets me with a nod and a smile.

"Good morning, my dear."

"Good morning," I reply.

I find a seat on a comfortable chair and slowly sip
my coffee.

"No sunning by the pool today?" asks Corey,
looking at my dress.

I usually don't wear anything but swimsuits these
days. Today I want a change.

"Maybe later," I say.

"Hm."

"Late night at the office?" I ask, watching how his

expression switches from content to conflicted.

It is no matter. He will be dead soon. I just have to wait a little while after the shock of Brad's disappearance settles. After my fruit salad breakfast, I go to the pool and stare at the water. Someone died in its depths because of me. I am like a fierce queen who protects her castle from unworthy intruders. I can't help but smile at that. Everything I want is almost in my grasp. All I need to do is rid myself of Corey. I can't be a true queen until I kill the king.

I look forward to seeing what sort of home Steve lives in. I want to criticize everything about his house in front of him just because I can. I grin at the thought. If he annoys me, I might kill him, too. First, I go to the mall to buy a few new outfits for the upcoming week. I need a dress for a Wednesday breakfast with the pilots' wives that I agreed to go to and a little black dress for the gala on Saturday night. I can't say I have ever felt happy about anything. I am not like most fools who exist in this world. I rarely feel things other than anger or annoyance, but when I try on beautiful clothes, I feel an air of whimsy. I take a turn

about the room and admire myself in the mirrors.
After the mall, I stop by a trendy lounge close to
Steve's house to order a drink before going over. I
want to feel a buzz that will take the edge off any
disappointments that the visit may bring.

Steve's home is a bungalow with heated floors,
chandeliers, an elevator, modern décor, and pure
white paint on the walls. He's had his cook prepare us
a delicious meal of lemon chicken with a side of beets
sprinkled with goat cheese. We sit down at the table
and the conversation is mediocre, but not murder-
inducing. I am not surprised that he takes little interest
in my daily routine. We exist in life to get what we
want. He has his way. I have mine.

After dinner comes the alcohol. We sit on his
comfortable leather couch sipping on dessert wine.
His disposition is quiet like mine. We talk about a
documentary that we both watched about wild animals
behaving out of character. It is one of the more
interesting conversations I've had this month. We
don't talk about anything to do with murder.

"You have a nice place," I admit.

I'll give credit when it's due. He has relatively decent taste.

"Sometimes complex minds prefer simpler designs," he says.

"Indeed."

After the third glass, I slide my dress's straps down my shoulders. I inch toward him as I play with my rose gold necklace. Gazing at my neck, he licks his lips. Steve is a neck and collarbones guy. I know this, because that is where he tends to look the most when he is with a pretty woman at a party.

"You're stunning," he says.

I stand and slowly take off my dress, watching as his attention go to my black padded bra. He sets his glass down and takes off his shirt. He has a lean physique that has been naturally tanned by the sun. My body has craved the touch of someone else since settling down with boring, passionless Corey.

After he takes off his pants, I straddle him. I can see his arousal beneath his black Calvin Klein boxers. He grabs my round derriere with both hands as I slowly pull his underwear down. He grins wickedly at me and I don't hate the playfulness in his expression. It has been a while since I have genuinely had fun with someone else.

"I want to see you," he says, unclasping my bra.

He stares at my bare breasts.

"Beautiful," he says, grasping them gently.

Being small and firm, they are very sensitive to his touch. I moan as a slow burning arousal comes over me. He pinches my hard nipples then sucks on them. Before I lose my mind, I take his hard member into my hand and stroke him. I bite his neck, determined not to be fully taken by him.

He suddenly pushes me back on the couch and gets on top of me. I grit my teeth and remind myself that I am the one who is paying him for doing me a favour. I will do his bidding this time, but if this were my house, I would take the top position.

"You bit me," he rasps in my hear. "Now I will have to make you pay for that."

"Then do it," I taunt.

We have hot, rough sex then I leave.

I step through the front door of my own house just before midnight. Corey will probably be asleep. I am grateful that I demanded to have separate rooms. I like having things a certain way and his snoring is obnoxious at times. I don't want to kill him out of psychotic anger. I need to do it cleanly and with a clear head. There is no point in ruining quality sheets with his blood. Of course, he was hurt that I didn't want to sleep in the same bed as him unless we have sex, but he complied. I always get what I want from him.

I take a quick shower, change into a night gown, and slide beneath the silk sheets of my bed. I turn off the lamp and relax. The darkness is where I feel the most comfortable. I am home there.

The moment I fall asleep, all I see is water. I hear tiny waves lapping against the light blue pool liner. It is gently rippling as something struggles in it. Darkness quickly blots out the day and the water glows beneath a silvery moon. The peaceful setting is disturbed when a body is pushed into the pool, creating a loud splash and waves. I don't want to look at the scene all over again. I don't care about it. It's over and done with. I want the black to take this annoying sight away and allow me to sleep.

I am suddenly in the dark waters. Something glows beneath me. I don't want to look, but I do. I am entrapped by this dream and I might as well swim to whatever it is that is glowing. I move my limbs so I can swim deeper, intrigued until I come face to face with Brad's ghost. His skin glows the same as it did beneath the moon after I drowned him. His eyes aren't lifeless like they were that night. The intelligent brown orbs stare at me as we both sink to the bottom of the pool. My feet feel like they are filled with lead.

"You murdered me, but I'm not dead," he says.

His voice sounds exactly like it should under water. Muffed and strange.

"Yes, you are. I killed you."

I hate him even more than I did before. How dare he enter my dreams?

"I am not dead," he snarls, pushing me away from him.

"This is just a stupid dream!" I shout.

His angered expression softens for a moment before a wicked smirk lifts the corners of his mouth. He floats away while staring at me.

"I don't care about you, Brad!" I shout after him.

I push my feet off the bottom of the pool and swim for the water's surface. My lungs feels heavy as I pump my legs and arms. I reach desperately for the air, but I do not break through the water's barrier. I flail as my lungs begin to burn. I scream in anger, in pain. Is this how it feels to drown?

"Let me out!" I cry.

I awaken in a cold sweat surrounded by darkness. I am back in my soft bed gasping for air. I rarely have such vivid dreams. It doesn't matter. Brad is dead.

4

I kick the black punching bag with all my might. It swings away and I kick it again before it comes back to hit me. I bend my knees and punch it until I can't anymore. Panting, I take a step back to catch my breath and take a drink of water.

"Whoa girl. Everything okay?" asks Jimmy, my personal trainer.

I wipe the sweat off my face with a face towel. It is rare for me to sweat so much, but I am feeling the rage today. I glance over at him. He is grinning.

"I'm fine," I say.

"If you say so," he says with a skeptical look on his face.

I hate his attempts to make conversation with me, but he's a damn good fitness trainer. He got me in perfect shape for my wedding day and I've stuck with him since. He comes to my house three days per week willing to torture my body in the most effective ways possible. I've never tried boxing in my life, but after that strange dream, I've been in need of an outlet for my rage. Boxing seemed to be the right thing. Good thing Corey already has a punching bag installed in our home gym.

Jimmy shows me how to do a proper upper cut and jab. I repeat the actions with vigor. He seems impressed with my efforts and I feel the burn. We are both satisfied with the session.

After my trainer leaves, I wash the sweat off in the shower and decide to put on a bikini so I can sit out by the pool with a new magazine. It will be peaceful out there this time. I shift uncomfortably in the chair as I flip through the first few pages. It is time to get a new chair, among other things.

"I need a whole new life," I say quietly.

I grit my teeth and throw the magazine at the glass door. It doesn't quite make it, adding another edge to my annoyance. I pace around the pool, glancing at the still waters before looking at the garden. The rake and shovel Brad used the other day lean against the fence. He didn't have the decency to put them back in the shed. He really was just a freeloader pretending to work. Good thing I got rid of him.

"Marie, honey," calls Corey as he opens the sliding door.

"I thought you'd be at the airport by now," I call back, feeling poked by his presence.

"I'm running late because I haven't heard back from Brad. He should have been here by now. Have you seen him?"

"No. I haven't seen him since yesterday morning."

Corey shakes his head with a frown. "It's not like Brad to be this late and not call ahead to let me know."

He seems shaken. I will never understand why the guy cares so much about a dumb kid he barely knows.

"You're not going to miss work over this are you?" I ask in exasperation. "Are you two fucking or something?"

Corey fires me a caustic look before closing the door. I pay him back with a cold look. He looks away from me and disappears. He'll be dead soon. No matter.

I am agitated that another relaxing afternoon by the pool is spoiled. I walk around the rectangular reservoir. It looks so peaceful that one could forget how deadly it can be. A sudden gust of wind brings some prematurely fallen leaves into the water. I watch the ripples that form in the water as a result. The memory of Brad sinking below the water's surface comes back to my mind's eye.

"No," I say sharply. "I don't care about him. I don't give a fuck about anyone."

I shake my head. Brad. What a fool for trying my patience the way that he did. He'd still be alive if he minded his own business. Now he's gone and I'll have to deal with Corey sulking about it until I kill him. I would have given my husband a little more time, but since he's going to ruin my peace over a missing pool boy, I'll have to act quickly. I wonder why I can't have a life free of assholes.

My pulse quickens and I cannot still the rage any longer. I look back at the garden and run over to it. I grab the shovel and stab the soil with it. I start to hack at the ground, destroying flowers and uprooting entire plants. My anger is boiling over and I just want to kill someone.

"You asshole!" I scream. "Fuck you!"

I toss the shovel at the fence and it hits the stained wood, leaving a mark. I stand there trembling, overcome by anger at the sandy-haired pool boy who made me kill him.

I walk away and take deep, slow breaths. I step into the house as Corey is going out the door.

"Corey, we need to upgrade our backyard. I'd like to hire a landscaper to spruce it up."

He gives me a look and I think it is one of disgust. "Whatever you want, dear."

I pout. "Why are you brushing me off like this, Corey? I was thinking we could have a garden party next month with all your work friends. It would be an event they'll thank you for repeatedly. I'll make sure it's grandiose and unforgettable."

He exhales loudly. "Do what you want. I have to go."

I watch him drive off. What a dismissive defeatist. He'd never stand up to me even if his life depended on me. Too bad he isn't a little smarter.

I browse local landscaping companies on Google and find one with the best reviews. I can't set foot in that backyard until it has been revamped. I also want the water in the pool changed. The thought of touching the same water that I used to drown my victim disgusts me. I need to start fresh. I deserve to.

I give the landscaping company with the best reviews a call to get a price estimate and to see when they are available to start working on the yard. The level of work that I want done will require a lot of manpower. It turns out they are unable to accommodate my needs in the time frame that I want; I hang up on them. I tell myself to give them a 1-star review on Google later.

I feel restless as evening approaches. I am sick of this house. Everything about it bores me now. I need a different life. I am so close to starting afresh, but it will take a little more work to get there. Corey will be home tomorrow night. I'll do it then. I can kill him the same way that I killed Brad then I will call Steven again to help me with the body. His only requirement for payment will be more sex. I like the way he fucks.

I put on my favourite satin black nightgown and get into my bed. I hesitate before turning off the light and question why I do it. I've never, ever been afraid of the dark - not even as a child. It must be all the annoyances of the last two days filled with stupid people. They are making me feel stranger than usual. I remind myself that it's been years since I've killed someone. I just need to get back into the swing of things. Soon this place will be a distant memory and I will be on my own again living in true freedom.

I smile. Everything will be fine. I reach over and turn off my lamp.

-5-

The peaceful darkness is shattered by bright lightning.
I am lying in my bed as I wake up, but I sense
something hovering over me. I can't move as buzzing
fills my ears; I can't close my eyes as a glowing object
forms before me. I try to open my mouth to shout at it
to fuck off, but my teeth feel like they are sealed shut.
The brightness begins to take the form of a man. The
male figure is slim and lean. I don't want to look
anymore. I want to get up off my bed and kick him in
the face.

Planted on my mattress, the buzzing intensifies as
the face of the dreamlike man takes form. It is Brad
and he is shining like the surface of the moon. I long
to scream and break free of the hold on me, but my
efforts are in vain. I don't understand what is
happening. I am forced to look at the idiot's gloating
expression as he moves closer to me. I don't believe in
ghosts so he can't be returning from the under world
to seek vengeance on me. I rationalize what could be

happening in my brain as he steps slowly toward my
bed. He is smirking. It's that look all men have when
they have you cornered and there is nothing you can
do to get away. I want to grab a sharpened knife so
badly.

My heart pounds against my breastbone. I would
slit his throat and gut him if I could. My pulse races so
quickly that my eardrum thunders and drowns out the
sickening buzzing sound.

Brad's apparition reaches my bed; he bends until
his face hovers over mine. It isn't real. I've never
believed in ghosts. Whatever it is I am seeing causes
chills to from at the back of my head and whisper
down my spine. Nothing has ever given me fear like
this. What the hell is going on with my head?

"How do you like being the helpless one, you
murdering little bitch?" he asks.

I know exactly how it feels to be at someone else's
mercy. I want to kill him all over again, but I am as
useless as a china doll in my current state. All I can do
is watch this figment of my imagination as it tries to
toy with me. He grins wickedly and sticks his tongue,

lowering his face enough to lick my forehead. I feel
hot all over as the desire to hurt him overcomes me. I
know he's not real, but it feels real.

"I am going to kill you for killing me," he hisses.

I struggle with all my might to open my mouth. I
try to move with every fibre of strength I possess, but
it is impossible.

Suddenly, it is dark again and I am alone in my
room. The nightmarish vision of Brad has vanished.
The heaviness in my head lifts and I sit up quickly,
clawing at the lamp until my finger hits the switch. In
the light, I shudder. I check my phone. It is 5:05 AM.
I feel oddly cold.

I jump out of bed and take a hot shower. What is
going on with my brain? Nothing like this has ever
happened to me. I don't care about what I did to Brad.
He's just another idiot who got in my way. I never
want to think about him again.

I leave the shower and walk up to the foggy mirror.
I run my hand over the glass and see myself in the
blurred reflection. I study my eyes. They look empty
as they should. I am aware of how little I care for

other people. I was created to be better than others - I am smarter, more beautiful, more fashionable, more cunning. It is why I have been gifted with the knowledge of how to get ahead of others. I need to preserve my own existence and rid the world of idiots. I think of Brad's eyes and how warm they used to be when he would look at me. His kindness is what killed him. I hate soft things. He made the wrong choice to work for my husband.

"You bastard," I hiss as I style my hair.

I am shocked at myself for forgetting to wash, tone, and moisturize my face before drying and flat ironing my hair. There is something wrong with me. My memory never slips like that.

"I need help."

After getting dressed and applying my makeup, I rush out the door and jump into my black Audi R8. I drive to the general hospital. When I walk through the automatic doors, I search out the mental health wing on the hospital map and walk there. I step past the people waiting in emergency. They glare at me for making an annoying sound with my high heels on the hard floor; I smirk. Their discomfort is my glee. I stifle a laugh and walk up to the front desk of the mental health department. An unremarkable woman with a mullet-like hairstyle and cheap foundation settling into her wrinkled face greets me.

"Hi receptionist," I say. "I need to make an appointment with a psychiatrist today."

Her eyes widen as she rolls her chair backward. "You do realize there's a waiting list to see the doctor, right? You will have to make an appointment."

I stare at her. This is not acceptable. She brings her attention to the outdated desktop computer she's using and clicks through the booking system.

"What's your schedule like, Ma'am?" she asks. "I could book you in as early as next Friday."

"That's over a week from now."

Her eyes glaze over. "That's the best I can do."

She doesn't care about my needs. What a shitty receptionist for a place that's supposed to help people with mental health issues. Clearly, I am above the other types of people she usually deals with. I am intelligent and I know how to get ahead in life. I just need help with this little hallucination issue I seem to be having.

"You'll have to do better," I say. "I need to see someone today. I am losing my sanity and I can't afford for it to get worse over the next week. Is there not a cancellation you can squeeze me into? I know people with mental health issues can be terribly unreliable."

I glance over my shoulder at the three people sitting in the waiting room chairs. They cast me weary glances.

The receptionist sighs deeply. "Let's see here."

I cross my arms and wait. If she doesn't fit me in, I will want to storm into one of the doctor's offices and demand that they accommodate me. The lady shakes her head and tells me again I will have to make an appointment for another day.

I take a deep breath to stifle my anger. Those stacks of paper on her desk would look so much better tossed all about the room, but I need to remain calm and courteous or they won't want to help me. I can't make demands. I need to play nice here.

"Very well," I say coolly. "May I at least use the washroom before I go?"

"Of course. It's down the hall to your left."

"Thank you."

My face hurts from fake smiling. After checking my makeup and hair in the washroom's mirror, I quietly exit the washroom and wander further down the hall. Most of the office doors are closed, but one is left half open. I peer inside. A middle-aged man with dark hair and black-rimmed glasses leans over his desk reading something. I walk in with a wide smile on my face. Noticing me, he sits up.

"Good day," I say pleasantly. "I know I don't have an appointment, but I really need to see someone. My mental health is in jeopardy as we speak."

He glares at me with his dark blue eyes. "You have to make an appointment, Ma'am. I am not seeing any clients today."

"Oh," I say, slouching my shoulders and pouting in just the right way. "The receptionist wasn't able to get me in today. I was really hoping to get some help from a doctor."

The psychiatrist brings a hand to his forehead as he exhales sharply. "What seems to be the problem, Miss ..."

"My name is Marie. You must be Dr. Fitzgibbon if the sign on the door is correct."

"I am, Marie. Sit down and tell me what the issue is. I can spare fifteen minutes, but you'll need to make an appointment for a full assessment and diagnosis. Do you understand?"

"Yes, Doctor," I say sweetly, sitting down in the chair on the other side of his desk. "I had a lifelike dream early this morning. Something like this has never happened before so you can imagine how scared I felt. I was wide awake, but I couldn't move as a glowing presence came at me. Then it turned into a man. Someone I used to know who died. I was paralyzed and couldn't open my mouth."

"Hm," he says.

"Doctor, I don't believe in ghosts and all that spiritual nonsense, but I wonder what is going wrong with my head. I rarely have dreams. Having one that was so lifelike this morning was very strange for me."

He clears his throat and leans forward. "It sounds like you were experiencing sleep paralysis."

I blink. That doesn't sound good. "What is that and how do I get rid of it? How did I catch this paralysis in the first place?"

"It is not something you can catch or cure. Sleep paralysis is sometimes an underlying symptom of narcolepsy, but if you have never been diagnosed with that condition, it is probably a sign of stress."

"Stress," I repeat. "So, there is no cure?"

"The best treatment for sleep paralysis is ensuring that you keep good sleeping habits and reduce your level of stress. Has something significant happened in your life lately?"

"I usually sleep well. My life is very easy, you see. I'm a trophy wife."

He chokes back a laugh. "You didn't answer my question. Has something occurred in your life that has stressed you out more than usual?"

"No. Not that I can think of," I lie.

"Sometimes, something in our subconscious can come out to play in the form of nightmares or waking dreams like you described. I don't believe these are a cause of great concern. As you mentioned, it's not a ghost or a spirit, it's just a figment of your imagination. As troubling as they seem in the moment, they're never dangerous and they go away within seconds."

"This sleep paralysis means I'm not going crazy, then?"

He shakes his head. "No. You are not crazy. It's something that happens to many people at least once in their lifetime."

He checks his watch and looks at me hollowly. "My time's just about up. You are more than welcome to book a full session with me another day. I should have some time next Friday."

I nod. "Thank you for taking the time to explain this to me, Doctor. I'll see myself out now."

He leans back in his chair and studies me with an unreadable expression on his face. "Have a good day, Marie."

6

As I drive home, a weight lifts off my shoulders. I am still just as in control of myself as I was before. Sleep paralysis is not that serious; it is just caused by stress. The only stressful thing in my life right now is Corey. Once he's dead, my sleep will be dark and dreamless. I will be back to my usual self soon.

Corey will be away until the evening, so I have the entire day to prepare his murder down to the last detail. I haven't felt so excited about something in a while. I will laugh all I want after his body is discarded and I am far away from this bland old house. Before going through a rehearsal of how I will execute my killing, I go to the kitchen and make a berry and frozen yogurt smoothie to energize my body. I avoid looking out the glass door to the backyard. It isn't fit to be seen. I can't believe I even bothered to think of redesigning it. It is a lost cause. I sit at the table and bask in the silence as I drink the nourishing preparation.

I walk about the house imagining Corey walking through the door and how I will act when he arrives. I will lead him outside to look at the stars like we did on our first date. He will fall for the chance to have a nostalgic romantic moment with me. Then I will stick him with the needle and push him into the pool. Once I am out, I'll never have to look at it or think about it again. I practice how the interaction with Corey will go several times under different scenarios. If he is against going outside, I will seduce him in his bedroom - or I will take him in mine. I am confident that no matter how he reacts to me when he's home, I will have him wrapped around my little finger in no time. Either way, he will die tonight.

I kill the time by doing a home cardio workout designed by my personal trainer. I repeat the routine for good measure. Then I shower and moisturize myself from head to toe. I slip into one of my other red dresses. The mermaid style one that I murdered Brad in won't do. A woman who has good taste never wears the same outfit to the same type of event. What a shame Corey will never get to see me in it. His loss.

I do my nails on the hour before I expect my husband to come through the door. I paint them crimson so they match my gown.

When I hear the door open, I walk calmly out of my room holding my silver sparkly purse that has the bottle of ketamine and syringes inside of it. A strange voice fills the air as I make my way to the top of the staircase. I stop and look below at the doorway where Corey and a blond guy are talking in hushed tones. I resist the urge to swear loudly. This is unbelievable.

"Dear, who is that?" I call.

Both turn to face me. My heart nearly stops as I look at the strangely familiar face. He looks almost exactly like Brad, but he is a couple of years younger.

"I'm here to see what happened to my brother," says the boy indignantly.

"I told him we haven't seen Brad for a couple of days and we are worried," says Corey, looking from me back to Brad's brother.

I slowly descend the staircase feeling the hatred for my husband intensify. How dare he let that kid come so close to our home? He has ruined another perfect murder with his shitty timing. I stifle my rage and plaster a smile on my face.

"Welcome," I say to Brad's little brother. "What might your name be?"

"I'm Alex. So, tell me. Where the hell is my brother?"

He looks at me as though I should know.

"Why, I hardly said two words to Brad," I say calmly. "He seems like a nice boy, but I'm just the housewife. Corey is the one who hired and paid him."

"Haven't you tried calling his cell? Or have you asked his friends about him?" asks Corey.

"He won't answer and no one knows where he is," says Alex, sounding frustrated.

His eyes dart back to me. They are unnervingly similar to Brad's. I shake off the strange feeling I get. This kind of stuff isn't supposed to bother me. Since when do I care about eyes?

"Brad did tell me something about you, Mrs. Robson, the last time we spoke," says Alex, moving through the doorway.

I cross my arms as I turn my nose up at him. "We did not give you permission to step into our home and I don't appreciate your tone."

Alex's eyes flicker in anger. "He told me that he caught you trying to drown a bunny in your pool."

I laugh darkly while they both stare at me.

"My wife would never do that," says Corey, shaking his head. "I'll do my best to try to track your brother down, but I really need to ask you to leave now."

Alex does not take his eyes off me. I refuse to look away even though his similarity to Brad is making the weight on my shoulders return. Just when I thought the stress in my life would soon be over.

"I'm on to you, Mrs. Robson," he says. "If I don't hear back from my brother in another day, you'll be sorry."

I smirk. "Now you're sounding ridiculous. Go home, little boy. If you threaten me again, I will call the police."

Corey pushes him outside and closes the door. Locking it, he gives me a sidelong glance.

"Is that true?" he asks.

"I don't want to know what you're asking me," I mutter, walking away from him.

The moment has deflated. I can't kill the annoying idiot with my mood dropping so low. I feel bile rise in my throat. Why can't I be allowed to forget about stupid Brad? In any event, his brother has nothing on me. Second-hand information about me trying to drown a small animal isn't going to be that incriminating. Brad will be eternally missing. No one can prove he is dead if there is no body to be found. Steve took care of that. The whole thing will blow over soon.

I look back at Corey. "It looks like you hired the wrong guy to be our pool boy."

"I don't regret hiring Brad. He's a good kid. Something must have happened to him."

I roll my eyes. "Good one, Sherlock."

"I'm going to bed. I can't deal with your coldness and negativity tonight," he says.

I watch him walk up the stairs. He sees me as cold and negative. My sweet persona isn't fooling him anymore. He knows there is something off about me. There goes my opportunity to sleep in peace. I could grab a knife and slit his throat in his sleep, but I would rather do it with a cool head. I'll have to wait a little longer to finally kill Corey.

Howling sounds in the distance, overpowering the silence. The wolves are close again. I make my way up to the room to retire for the night when a sharp yelp breaks the quiet. It sounds like it came from the street. Feeling a little restless in the wake of my failed murder plan, I venture outside and turn the porch light on. I don't see anything. I step further and movement from the road catches my attention. I walk to the end of my driveway and see the silhouette of a scrawny dog. Seeing me, it limps toward me. As it comes into the light, its brown eyes look helplessly into mine. He is a discarded dog seeking food and shelter.

"How cruel life can be to the weak," I say.

I back away slowly, not wanting to turn my back to it in case it becomes aggressive. Its brown eyes widen as I distance myself from it. It whimpers and yelps again. It looks so pathetic that I don't see why anyone would want to help it. The beast would be better off getting hit by a car.

I spin around and sprint for the house, quickly closing the door behind me. I go up to my room and take another hot shower. Feeling warm and drowsy, I fall into bed and sleep takes me soon after.

The night sends me into a spiral of abstract dreams. Alex walks toward me in a foggy reality with the injured homeless dog at his side. Both of their gazes are dark and sad. I want to run away from the fools, but I am stuck in place, paralyzed. They do nothing except stare at me. As I leave that dream, I am greeted by a blueish face with chocolate-coloured eyes. Brad.

"No," I say, shaking my head. "You need to leave my mind. I want you to get out!"

He grins wide.

"You're dead! You are aren't real."

He shakes his head. "Cold-hearted bitch."

"My heart isn't cold, it's empty."

He sneers at me as bright pink lights mar my vision of him. He floats away and I struggle to get out of there. Before I make my way out of the large, blurry room, he grabs me by the wrist and pulls me toward him.

"Get lost, asshole!" I scream.

"Why did you kill me?" he demands.

I try in vain to move away, but his grip on my wrist tightens.

"Tell me," he presses.

"Because you were in the way."

There. I said it. He bares his teeth and takes a bite into my neck. I feel flesh and tissue being torn out.

I wake up yelling in the darkness. That bastard. I don't understand how to get him out of my head. These dreams need to stop. My door starts to slowly open. I sit up, on edge. Corey stands there.

"Bad dream?" he asks.

I nod. "It's fine. I'll just make a tea and go back to sleep."

"Did you do something to Brad?" he asks bluntly.

I shake my head. "How could you think that of me?"

"I don't know. You never liked him. His brother seemed pretty convinced about the story of you drowning rabbits in the pool. Why would Brad make something like that up?"

There is strange buzzing in my ears as he talks. I feel an odd presence lurking above me; horrible gooseflesh covers my skin as I get up.

"I don't appreciate your tone," I say, brushing past him. "Or your accusations."

"I'm not accusing you. I'm just trying to talk to you about this."

"Spare me."

He should be dead, but there he is interrogating me about stupid Brad. I walk down the stairs, desperate for fresh air, but not wanting to appear like I am. It will make me look insane.

"Marie?" calls Corey.

"Give me a minute!" I call.

The outside air cools my skin as I step out the door and to the porch. The twinkling stars fleck the sky so beautifully. I ask myself why I don't admire them more often. Our home is half an hour away from the big city, so we get a decent view of the sky. I walk down my driveway, keeping my eyes fixed on the starry firmament above me. It's not like me to be so affected by nature. I think the doctor was too hasty to dismiss my condition as being caused by stress. There is something wrong with my head. I am not myself.

Soft whimpering interrupts my musing. A shadowy, four-legged figure trots up to me. The injured dog has returned. He is only a few feet away from me. Somehow even he has entered my world. I have never liked animals.

"You pathetic thing," I say, shaking my head.

He steps closer, looking hopefully into my eyes.

"I'd rather crush you than help you," I snarl, starting to turn away, but bumping into a solid body.

It is Corey. He is a head taller than me and solidly built. I am very aware of that fact as I look up at him. He looks down at me with a disgusted expression. For the first time since I met him, I wonder if he will hurt me.

"I heard what you said to that dog. You really are a cold bitch, aren't you?"

They never get it right. I am empty, not cold.

"You want to take this filthy animal into our house, do you?" I ask, looking back at the foul-smelling mutt.

"Why are you like this, Marie?" asks Corey.

When the dog realizes that he has my attention again, the animal walks up to me and noses my hand with his cold, dirty snout. I grit my teeth as the urge to smack him in the head overcomes me. I stop myself from doing it for my own sake. If I fall any further from Corey's good books, he might start to think I killed Brad.

"We can take him in for the night then I can drive him to the shelter tomorrow morning before I go to the airport," says Corey, bending down to pet the dog's head.

"Fine," I say with a tired sigh. "Let him in the house. See if I care."

I step back to the house. The mongrel rushes past Corey to follow me. I wonder why he likes me so much. I thought dogs could sense bad people. I look over my shoulder at Corey's perplexed face before walking inside.

7

I sit at the kitchen table on my laptop as Corey bathes the stray in the bathroom. I look up Alex Smith on Facebook after discovering Brad's last name. I found it by looking in Corey's chequebook. My husband is old school in that way, preferring paper transactions over e-transfer. I discover a lot of useless details about Alex, but one interesting thing about him is that he is a foster kid. He is living at a group home. Out of curiosity, I research everything I can about it. It doesn't look like the nicest place to live. He must be a pretty depressed kid living in that shitty arrangement. I wonder for a moment if Brad was from a similar background - being passed around to different foster parents until he aged out of the system. I find Brad's profile on Alex's friends list. His profile picture is smiley. I should have known he was compensating for depression and a bad upbringing. No one in life is ever really that happy. He looks like one of those portrait models on the sheets of paper they put in picture frames. I check out his wall and there are a few people asking what happened to him.

"I happened," I say.

"You okay, Marie?" asks Corey.

The sound of claws on smooth hardwood flooring draw my attention to the dog. He is clean and his fur is damp. He doesn't look so bad without mud and matted fur taking away from the corn silk colour of his coat. He sits next to Corey with a wide smile on his face as he pants. He looks like he's part golden retriever.

"He smells better," I remark.

"It took me half an hour just to brush out the mats in his fur, but he took the bathing with dignity. His paw looks like it's strained. Nothing is broken."

"Lucky him. At least he won't stink up the place now."

"You didn't answer my question."

"About what? If I am okay?"

"Yeah."

I just want him to go away, but he's standing there staring at me like a brute.

"I don't know. Life is weird sometimes."

"You can say that again."

He finally breaks out of his trance and goes to the fridge to take out some boxed leftovers from our various nights out at restaurants.

"You like chicken and rice, buddy?" he asks the dog.

He carefully strips the chicken bones of meat and then puts the box on the floor. The dog devours the food.

"Well, I'll see you later then," says Corey, looking from the mutt to me. "I'll be off early tomorrow. I won't be back for a few days. My flights will take me to Seattle."

"Oh, you're taking the dog with you in the morning, right?"

He runs a hand through his dark hair. "Yeah I'll take him. Unless you're okay to keep him here for a few days."

"What? Why would I want a stray dog in our house?"

He rolls his eyes. "I thought so."

He goes upstairs shaking his head. I glare at him thinking he is lucky he hasn't been murdered by me yet.

I turn my attention back to Brad's Facebook profile. He doesn't have much on there. Just a few pictures and the high school he graduated from. He didn't even put in the university he was attending.

I close the window and start to do some online shopping. I need some new outfits and I feel like browsing for some inspiration. As I look at clothes on Neiman Marcus's website, the mongrel inches closer to me.

"Oh, you want to get close to a psychopath, do you?" I coo sarcastically.

He doesn't seem unnerved by my cold tone. What a strange animal. He must have come from a pretty horrible life if he wants to please me. Usually animals, especially dogs and cats, stay well away from me. I have no desire to pet him or engage in any activity with him. I continue scrolling through different fashion sites while he sits quietly watching me. I realize it is almost two in the morning by the time I get bored with shopping.

I stand up to stretch then suddenly the dog's ears perk up. He trots past me and stares out the window, growling. I am slightly intrigued to see what he finds so interesting. I turn off the kitchen light so I can peer outside. Movement catches my attention and the dog's. He starts barking. I try to follow the moving body with my eyes, but it's so dark that it distorts my view of who or what it is. I grab a sharpened kitchen knife off the kitchen counter and open the door to get a better look at who I need to call the police on.

The dog rushes out the door and into the inky darkness barking like a rabid beast. I realize the futility in telling the idiot to stop barking, so I walk outside. A slim figure in a hoodie and track pants does a run jump at the fence and climbs over it.

"Hey!" I call.

I bolt for the gate and see it's already open. I run out and the dog follows me before racing ahead. The sound of running footsteps and the maniacal barking shake up the night's stillness. This is working out to my advantage; the dog could easily catch up to my unwelcome guest and make him stumble. The shadowy figure flees to the woods and the dog chases him, but it's an awkward run because of his sprained foot. Still holding my knife, I jog after them into the dark forest. The moon is not out tonight. I will have to rely on my eyes adjusting to the dim. Despite my strange dreams, the dark does not bother me. Terrible things happen at all times of the day. Whoever I am pursuing is afraid of being caught. He is in the wrong and I am in the right. I have the upper hand and I am not afraid.

I listen for the sound of the hooded trespasser or the dog. It has gone quiet. I hope the dog takes him down. My mouth waters as I imagine toying with him. My grip tightens on the weapon in my hand.

A chorus of wolf howls shatter the momentary silence. I freeze. They are too close. I start back home walking as lightly as possible. I know that I am being paranoid, but I would rather not tempt fate. I walk a little faster. Home isn't far away, though it seems to take a lot longer getting back there than it did to reach the woods.

Growling sounds close by. I look back expecting to see the mutt with a piece of the coward's clothing in his mouth. Instead, I see nothing but darkness.

I know something is there. I step backward to see if it creates a reaction. That is when I see movement in the distance. Wolves. Their paws patter on the ground as they move toward me.

I move in the direction of the river as my heart beats so hard I wonder if it will explode out of my body. I have my knife. I can slit the throats of the ones that get too close. They don't run at me. Instead, they inch forward and hover for a few moments. They must sense my aggression.

My gaze rests on the largest member of the pack as I keep moving toward the tributary. He seems to be the leader as the others follow him. He is weighing his options like I am. The water is close. The singing rapids fill my ears. I relax. I am so close that I can sprint for the water and jump in if I need to.

A sharp yelp breaks the silence and the wolves break into a run toward me. I look away from the shadowy four-legged figures and pump my legs as I move faster than I ever have in my life. Once I am at the riverbank, I jump into the icy water. The shock of being submerged in cold, rushing water makes me lose my breath. I let go of the knife in my hands and swim with all my might to reach the water's surface. My head breaks the watery barrier and I cough into the air. I suck in a deep breath and try in vain to fight against the strong current.

The water carries me so fast and my skin feels so numb from the icy temperature. I take a big breath of air before the water pulls on my long legs, forcing me under. I fight to keep my head above the surface, but the force of nature wins. My muscles burn as I struggle. The water is dark, chilling. It runs so fast that it doesn't seem real. My lungs are on fire and I can no longer hold my breath. My shoes graze the muddy bottom of the river; I can't move my limbs. I am being dragged like a piece of heavy driftwood.

Something bright breaks through the pitch black. All I can do is watch as the glowing form of the boy I killed floats toward me. He shakes his head at me with a smirk.

"Tsk tsk," he says.

I will die if I let out my breath. I can't talk; I can only listen.

"A cold death for a cold bitch," he says. "Maybe karma does exist."

He stops a few feet away from me.

My body feels like it is on fire with ice blue flames. He reaches for me with both arms and draws me close to him until our chests touch. He wraps his arms around me, tightening the hug, and brings his lips to my ear. "I just wanted to protect you, Marie. You have robbed me of my life. How am I supposed to be at peace with this?"

I can feel the pain in his garbled voice. He was needlessly murdered because he wanted to help me. Now I will drown just like he did.

"Give it one more try and see," he says, fading away.

I am surrounded again by the black void.

"Wait!" I cry, reaching out for him.

I breathe in water and it burns my nose and lungs like liquid nitrogen on bare skin. I choke and scream as the frigid fluid fills my airways. My feet are touching the bottom of the river. I focus beyond the suffocating agony and squat. With all my might, I push my feet off the floor and swim upward. White stars fill my vision and I suddenly feel very warm. When I am sure that my mind will fall into oblivion forever, my face rises above the water. I take in a desperate breath of air and swim weakly for the shore as I choke and puke.

The water is calmer downstream so it is easier to swim, but I can't see anything around me. For all I know, the wolves are waiting on land. Maybe the trespasser I chased is standing ashore with plans to kill me. I don't care so long as I get out of the water.

When my hands touch the mud in shallower waters, I cry out in relief. I feel like I am barely alive as my body shivers like a dry leaf in the wind. I force myself to stand on trembling legs and take clumsy steps until my feet leave the water. Exposed to the night air, a terrible wave of cold hits me. I walk on sand and grass then drop to my knees, shivering. I wrap my arms around myself. I have never been so frigid in all my life. A whimpering, four-legged creature approaches me from the ebony abyss. It is the stray.

He walks up to me wagging his tail. His wet tongue warms a small part of my face as he licks it.

"You came for me?" I ask raggedly.

The mutt nudges me with his head and I wrap my arms around his body. He feels like a toasty blanket. He doesn't move away as I shiver in the wretched darkness. I marvel at his loyalty. He lets me hold him, still licking my face and neck. I hug him tighter as an uncontrollable tidal wave of sadness hits me. It is so painful that a wretched sob escapes from the pit of my stomach.

"What is happening to me?" I cry.

I never feel sad and I definitely never cry. I am an empty shell of a woman, barely human, a cold-hearted killer, but right now I feel something so disturbing that I wonder if I am dying. For the first time in my life, I feel like someone is squeezing the life out of my heart. It seems like my chest will cave in as I think of Brad. Was his sickening kindness so genuine that it still lives on to torment me?

He is dead because of me. No matter how many times my mind resurrects his memory, he is never coming back to life. Only the ghost of him remains in my twisted mind.

I lean against the dog. He sits up tall and strong as I bury my face into his soft fur. The thought of walking back home in the darkness with hungry wolves in the woods makes me shudder, but I stand on shaking legs. My limbs feel like jelly, but I force myself to walk. I don't want to lie shivering by the water until dawn or death. I need to move in order to stay warm. The dog is at my side and he is alert. I can't recall anyone ever sticking by me after a difficult situation. An animal that I would have kicked and left to die in the darkness is being loyal to me. I marvel at this as we journey through the forest. This night is close to the worst one I have ever had, but I am not alone. I have a friend with me this time.

-8-

Every inch of my body aches. I turn over on the couch and look at the dog sleeping at my feet. Hearing me stir, his head lifts and he wags his tail. His warm, brown eyes turn to slits as he yawns. He hasn't left my side since I made it out of the river. The wolves didn't bother to go after me as I made my way back home. The murky waters must have washed off any scent that drew them to me in the first place. I smell like a fish. This is the worst I have ever smelled in my life.

I look groggily out the window. The sun is low on the blue horizon. It must be around six thirty in the morning. I only slept for a couple of hours. I sit up to stretch my sore muscles. I was so close to being dead. Like Brad.

I close my eyes as a dull pain inflicts my heart once again. Is this how people feel when they are sad? I wonder how they make it through life if they feel this way more than once.

A door opens and closes upstairs. I groan as Corey rushes down the stairs. At the sight and smell of me, he stops at the landing and stares.

"Marie, what the hell?"

"Long story."

He takes a step toward me and his eyes widen at the sight of my new companion lying at my feet. "I'm confused."

"Look, there was a guy who trespassed on our yard last night and I thought I'd go after him. I ended up chasing him all the way into the woods and then I fell in the river."

His eyes widen. "Are you okay? Marie, are you crazy?"

"I guess."

"I sometimes don't think I know you. Why would you run out alone into the night like that? You could have been hurt badly. That guy could've been violent!"

I laugh darkly. It turns out that guy was the least of my worries last night.

"You smell bad," he remarks.

I drop my head onto the soft couch and groan. "I was exhausted when I got in early in the morning. I couldn't make it upstairs to shower if my life depended on it."

"Why didn't you call me if you were all the way out there in the dark? You must have been freezing after falling into the water like that."

"I lost my phone in the river."

"Wow."

"You can say that again," I say, stretching again and wincing at a painful knot in my back.

"Well, I'll take the dog off your hands. The shelter is on the way to the airport, but I've got to leave now."

"Wait! I'll keep him."

"Are you serious?"

"Yes. I want to keep the dog."

Corey shakes his head. "You sure you're okay?"

I shrug. "I think it will be good to have him around here. He's very loyal."

"That's just like you, Marie. I go right, you go left. It's how it's always been with us. Fine. Keep the dog, but please take good care of him. He's a nice animal. I've gotta go. See ya."

He walks out the door and I sink into the couch again. I'll have to thoroughly clean the fabric once I'm showered and dressed. Washing myself should be the first thing on my itinerary for the day. No. I need to feed the dog before that. I rush over to the fridge and forage through the boxed leftovers, picking the one with mashed potatoes and roast beef. I heat it up quickly in the microwave then test the temperature by forking a small portion in my mouth. It doesn't seem too hot.

"I'll get you real dog food soon, boy," I promise.

I put the box on the floor; he devours it.

I rush upstairs to my bathroom and strip out of my smelly, muddy clothes. The hot water rushes over my skin and I wash my whole body twice to be sure the weird bog smell is off me. I wash my hair twice as well. I put on a hair mask and a face mask then bask in the warm, steamy room. I am grateful to be alive, but my brain is slipping. I am starting to feel things and I don't know how to fix that. I can't go to a psychiatrist for the issue. My sudden ability to feel empathy would be encouraged by mental health professionals.

I shudder despite the heat surrounding me. This is what hell must be. No one will help me find my sociopathy again. The world wants humans to feel pain and suffering, especially women. It doesn't want me to be numb to other's stupidity and pain. My kind is portrayed as monsters, mentally ill, psychopaths. I don't know what I'm supposed to do with these new feelings. They can't last forever. Like sleep paralysis, perhaps this ache in my chest is caused by stress and will go away in time.

I perform my skin care routine, style my hair, get dressed, and apply makeup to my face. Realizing it's been over two hours since I started pampering myself, I rush downstairs to see what the dog is up to. He is lying on the mat by the door. When he sees me approaching him, he trots up to me. I can't imagine doing anything but good to him. I lower myself to the floor so I am at face level with him then I gently pet his head. He pants happily.

"You were there for me last night. I'll never forget that."

A piercing shriek sounds from outside. I rise, already knowing what it is. I rush outside to the backyard that I swore I'd never look at again unless it was to drown my husband there. I jog over to the pool. Sure enough, a little rabbit has fallen in and is struggling to get out of the pool. The dog whimpers, pacing back and forth behind me, yelping every few seconds. I stare down at the little head and ears bopping about the water's surface. I have never felt anything more than a need to crush small things when I see them. It is so tiny and completely at my mercy as my hands hover above it. One part of me wants to push it under, but another part of me screams to help it like Brad did.

I bend down, cup my hands, and quickly lift it out of the water. It cries out, wriggles out of my grasp, and hops to the garden. The dog lazily chases it.

"Hey!" I call.

He returns to me wagging his tail. My heart is racing as I pet his golden head. There is something very wrong with me, but it doesn't feel half bad. I helped something that had absolutely no benefit to me. I have never done that before.

I feel a presence behind me. Surely Brad is not haunting me in broad daylight. That would be too much. I feel a shiver as I turn around. It is Steve and he is not smiling. I jump almost a foot off the ground. The dog barks at him, but doesn't leave my side.

"You scared the hell out of me! What are you doing here?" I cry.

I pet the dog's head without taking my eyes off Steve.

"People are talking about you, Marie."

"What are they saying?"

"A missing pool boy. Your odd, moody behaviour. Running into the forest at three in the morning with a knife. There's been a lot to talk about."

He's wearing faded blue jeans and a grey Henley shirt, but nothing about his character is casual. I wonder if my backyard intruder last night had something to do with him.

"How do you know about all this?" I press.

"It is my job to know about everyone in my circle," he says, taking a menacing step toward me. "I helped you erase someone from existence, but he's more well-known than I realized. Brad was popular with a lot of the guys on the soccer team. They want to know what happened to him. Your husband in particular will pay good money to find him."

I am not able to say anything, because I can't breathe. Steve is just like me. At least, I used to be like him. A killer who will do anything to get ahead. I know he doesn't care about me and there is no reason why he should, but I still feel anger about his betrayal.

He eyes me harshly. "Keep it together, Marie, or I will need to take care of this annoying issue you seem to be having."

He looks down at the dog. "I thought you hated animals."

"So did I. Listen, I think I'm going to be leaving soon," I blurt.

He nods. "It might be the best thing for all of us. I'd do it soon if I were you."

"Thanks for the warning."

His eyes light up as he takes a step toward me. I can sense the sadistic glee he is feeling. "Well, I hate killing beautiful women when I'd rather fuck them, but I'll do it if it's for the greater good."

That cold smirk of his would give anyone chills. I know the look. He is not bluffing. He will kill me if I don't get the hell away from here.

"Fair enough, Steve," I say. "I'll go."

"Good-bye, my lovely little Marie."

I grit my teeth. Shouting out a biting retort will only complicate things. He walks out through the gate. It is time for me to leave.

-9-

I drive my Audi out of the driveway for the very last time. I don't look back. My favourite gowns, lingerie, shoes, exercise outfits, and beauty products are in the back of my car. I have a sharpened and sheathed knife in my purse. I also brought along all my expensive jewelry to sell later. I am leaving everything else behind, because I hate packing.

My dog sits in the passenger seat happily looking out the window. It occurs to me that I haven't thought about killing Corey once all day. I just want to get away and begin a new life. Maybe I don't need to kill in order to start over again.

The first place I stop at is the bank. I withdraw everything out of my chequing account in cash so my husband can't freeze my funds when he finds out I left. I settle the teller's concerns about draining my account by telling him about my plight as an abused and lonely wife. It works.

I have one hundred thousand dollars in my

possession which will last me all of one year if I'm not careful. I'll need to find another income source soon, but that's not important in the moment. I just need to drive far away without being caught.

I look over at my golden-furred companion and decide that I will keep him with me no matter what happens.

"What should I call you?" I ask.

He perks up at the sound of my voice. I feel the corners of my mouth pull upward into a smile. I can't recall the last time someone made me smile. He is my hero. I don't know what I would have done out there in the dark woods by the river with the wolves so close without him there. His presence grounded me when I went through one of the most horrific experiences of my adult life.

"Hero," I say. "That will be your name."

His ears perk up. I think he likes it.

I recall the group home that Alex lives in since I am in his neck of the woods. Out of curiosity, I pull up to the building. I shudder involuntarily and ask myself why my body is reacting this way. Feeling for other people is so strange. I can't say I like it, but I don't think there is anything I can do to stop it. I get out of the car and take my purse. Hero yelps at me.

"I'll be back soon," I say, tapping the window in hopes of settling him down. "Be a good boy, Hero."

I feel the strangest dull ache in my stomach as I walk away from the car and hear him yelping again. I just want to walk up to the foster home of Brad's little brother before I leave the city behind forever.

Sharp voices draw my attention away from my thoughts. I round the corner and the two people that I see ahead cause me to stop in my tracks. Steve and Alex are both standing outside talking to one another. Their conversation sounds heated; it looks like their fight will soon escalate to something physical.

Steve shoves Alex into the brick wall. Not cool. I unsheathe my knife. They don't see me yet as they stare intently at one another.

"I warned you to stay out of this, kid, but you didn't listen. Marie's mutt could have caught you and then what would have happened? You would have jeopardized yourself once Marie caught up with you which would then incriminate me," says Steve in a patronizing tone. "Now I have to do what needs to be done."

So, it was Alex. I should have known.

"You asshole!" yells Alex, trying to fight back. "You're the one who contacted *me!*"

Steve shoves him into the brick wall again. I shouldn't care. This doesn't concern me. Still, as I watch Steve encircle Alex's neck with his hand I want to wipe that cruel smile off his face. Maybe the world needs to be rid of him. He is the sort to go out seeking drama. At least when I've killed in the past it was to erase drama. I step noiselessly toward them as Steve uses his superior strength to restrain his young victim.

I break into a sprint toward them. My eyes are fixed on Steve. I drive my knife into his side, but he leaps away from me, so the stab isn't deep enough. He bares his teeth as a dark red spot forms on the right side of his shirt.

"Stupid bitch!" he yells.

He draws his own knife as his mouth lifts in a wicked grin.

"You want to die, I see," he sneers.

Alex is leaning back into the building watching us in perplexed silence. He'll be safe for the time being.

Steve lunges for me, but I block him with a quick kick to his forearm, knocking him off balance. I spin around and drive my knife into his back, leaping away as his knife grazes my upper arm. I grit my teeth and focus past the pain, determined to see him fall. I know I can do this.

We glare at one another like two wolves fighting over their territory. I am no better than he is. I have killed without blinking, but I can't let him kill Alex.

"What has happened to you?" asks Steve as we circle each other. "You have lost your mind, Marie."

I swallow past a painful lump in my throat. I don't reply.

He smiles cruelly.

"Oh, I see it now. You can feel things. How precious."

"Yeah. Something like that."

He frowns. "That's very disappointing. You could have run off with all your husband's money and started fresh and I could have used you as a contact down the road. I hoped we could fuck sometimes. Now I have to kill you. I thought you were so much smarter than this."

"Or maybe I'll kill you!" I shout.

I take a run at him and try to knife him in the stomach, but he kicks me hard in the abdomen. Unexpecting the rapid kick, I fall backward and land on my ass. He doesn't hesitate to leap on me and bring the cold, sharp metal of his weapon to my throat. My warm blood drips down my neck and trickles onto the pavement.

"You've been caught, Marie," he whispers in my ear. "You played the game so well until you killed that pool boy. What's the matter? Is his ghost haunting you now?"

"I regret killing him," I reply, realizing there's no way out of his strong grasp.

He has me pinned against the cement. What will happen to Hero? I hope he'll bolt if Steve opens the car door. I shudder at the thought of my new friend being alone in the world all over again, but it would be better than being at the mercy of this asshole.

"Oh, this has been fun," he says softly, caressing my cheek with his other hand. "But now it's time for me to get on with the rest of my day."

I don't struggle. I don't move. He presses the knife a little harder against my neck. I gaze up at the blue sky, regretting how often I took it for granted. If there is a hell, I know I am going there. It amazes me how little I've cared about life in general until last night.

"Any last words?" he rasps into my ear.

"I just wish …"

"Ah!" shouts Steve, suddenly tumbling off me.

I sit up in shock. Alex is on top of him. His knife goes flying in the air and hits the cement with a clink. I jump to my feet and retrieve it. I stare at my own blood dripping from the blade. Alex is strangling him with all his might. Steve struggles against the angry teenager, but he is losing strength. The element of surprise worked in Alex's favour.

"Let me finish him," I say.

Alex looks up at me with red eyes. He does not lessen his grip on Steve's neck.

"Why the fuck are you helping me?" he shouts.

"Let me kill him! You don't want this on your record. My life is already tarnished. Let me take the fall."

Alex growls and releases Steve. I stand over the light-headed Steve, who is practically unconscious. I slit his throat with my knife then stab his heart with his. I feel nothing as I drop the weapons and walk away from him.

Alex is gaping at me.

"You didn't answer me," he says. "Why did you help me?"

"I didn't want you to die."

He squints as tears stream down his ruddy face. "You killed Brad! My innocent brother. Why did you do that?"

Steve must have told him I did it. The terrible ache returns to my chest and stomach. I killed someone who didn't deserve to die, someone who just wanted to help me. Well, maybe that was a lie. Brad was probably trying to get me to have sex with him, but he was not a bad person. He deserves to be alive right now.

I can't answer Alex's question, because I am unable to speak. A painful lump has formed in my throat.

Alex bends over as he lets out a guttural cry. It is the kind of sound that makes your blood want to curdle.

"I know I am a horrible person, Alex, but your brother's death will haunt me forever."

He shakes his head at me. "It will haunt you forever? I don't give a fuck. You're insane! I should kill you. Brad is gone because of you! What kind of person kills just for the hell of it? I could scalp you right now and dig out your brains while you're still breathing."

I cross my arms and glance back at the knives resting close to Steve's corpse. "I'd understand if you tried, but I won't let you do it."

I slowly step away from him. He doesn't follow me as I go back to my car. I can sense him wrestling with the desire to have a go at me, but he restrains himself.

He possesses a natural kindness that I will never know. I take a wad of cash from the money bag in the car.

Hero barks at me from the passenger seat. I quickly shut the door and walk back to Alex.

"What the hell is this?" he asks, visibly trembling.

"I know this doesn't erase what I've done, but I want you to have this. It's twenty thousand dollars."

He backs away. "I don't want your dirty money, bitch. I want to see your head roll off your body so I can dissect it!"

The grief in his eyes. It is horrifying. I can see that nothing can comfort him, not even a sum of money that could lift him out of poverty for a short time.

"I know you want me dead, but wouldn't it be better if you had this money? Take it, get yourself a good place to live far away from here or put it into a college fund. It's yours."

"This is all about appeasing your damned conscience, isn't it?" he spits. "Nothing is ever going to erase what you did to Brad! You are sick in the head. The only thing that can help you is the electric chair."

I sigh deeply. My patience is waning.

"I want you to have the money. Please, take it off my hands."

He clenches his fists. He wants to hurt me, but he won't. I marvel at his strength of character despite being so young. I wonder why I was born to be so different.

"I hope you die very soon," he says with a hoarse voice.

"I know you do."

"This is still a joke to you, isn't it?" he shouts. "Do you understand how alone I am now that he's gone? Brad is the only family I have. You took him away from me! If your soul burns in hell forever, it still won't be a just punishment for what you've done. I swear to God! I hope that the worst things happen to you in this life."

"Maybe they already have."

He balls a fist and nearly lifts his arm to sock me in the face, but he stops himself. "Yeah? Good. You deserved it," he says between clenched teeth.

My chest constricts. I felt sadness like him once when I was too small to understand the sick things that were happening to me. Unable to fight back the lake of tears I held back for decades, I fall to the cement. A sob explodes from deep within me and I start to weep. I can't stop. I lie on the pavement in emotional agony as Alex stares down at me.

"Will you ever kill again?" he asks.

I shake my head. "Never again."

"If I see your face after this, I will kill you."

I nod. "Why did you go after Steve when he was about to kill me?"

"He's the most threatening of the two of you. No offence. I wanted to eliminate him and then have a go at you if I could, but you didn't run when you had the chance. You stayed and helped me."

"I didn't want to see you get hurt, Alex."

He shudders then takes the twenty thousand dollars cash from me and walks away. Maybe he's a bit rougher around the edges than his older brother, but he will never be a murderer like me. He tries to do the right thing no matter how shitty he feels.

I force myself to stand, draw in a shaky breath, and rush back to my car. I look over my shoulder at Steve lying dead on the pavement and at Alex walking away with the money. I feel sick enough to vomit; I lean against the vehicle to get my bearings. I close my eyes and Brad's face appears. His sad brown eyes and vengeful smirk torment me. If only some part of his soul could still be alive and aware of the impact he has had on me. His kind face in my mind's eye is still so vivid. I wish I could touch him and tell him how much I want to do things differently.

"I am so sorry for what I did to you, Brad. If I could go back in time, I wouldn't have killed you. I would let you live."

He fades away until darkness takes his place. I open my eyes again and look up. The sky is blue and I am empty.

I get into my car and drive away with Hero at my side. I have no idea where I'm going to go, but I know that I will never kill anyone again. I gave my word to Alex and I have Brad to thank for that. His kindness stretched beyond the grave and stirred something inside of me that I didn't realize I had.

Loud sirens sound above my thoughts. I don't bother to look at the bright flashing lights in the rear-view mirror as I step on the gas.

Acknowledgements

Thank you, first and foremost, to my readers. Without you my stories would have no eyes. I am very happy that you chose to read this book and I hope you liked it!

I want to thank my designer, Adrijus, from Rocking Book Covers. You created a book cover design that suits this story's mood and aesthetic to a tee. I am pretty sure that Marie would approve.

I would also like to give a shout out to fellow indie authors Dean Tongue, Ksenia Anske, and Bernard Jan for inspiring me to continue writing for the love of it. Your books and positive social media presence is a great encouragement for me. Thank you!

About The Author

Sara Kjeldsen is Canadian author and tea addict who lives on Canada's beautiful west coast. She writes both novels and short stories in hopes of inspiring the reader to view life in a more open and empathetic way.

Other Published Works By Sara Kjeldsen

The Red Coat And The Redhead
Eve & Adam
The Broken And The Foolish
The Pup & The Pianist
She & The Wolf
Sally
A Season To Fight

Social Media

Twitter: @Sara_flower
Instagram: @authorsarakjeldsen

Printed in Great Britain
by Amazon

29965195R00056